Contents

6	Dear Reader
7	Hopes and Dreams
8	Lexa Profile
10	Bria Profile
12	Avery Profile
14	Sophina Profile
16	All About You
18	Word Creator
19	Moxie Girlz Magazine
20	I Am Me!
22	World of Words
23	Spot the Difference
24	Sophina's Guide to Amazing Animals
26	Animal Challenge
27	Odd One Out
28	Around the World in 80 Steps
30	Mystery Maze: Part One
40	Colour Count
41	Sweet Sudoku
42	Style Yourself
44	True or False
45	Avery's Amazing Adventure
46	Bria's Guide to Travel
48	Design of Dreams
49	Muddle and Match
50	Mystery Maze: Part Two
60	Perfection Planner
62	Devastating Detective Skills
64	Japanese Inspiration
66	Colour Crazy
68	Avery's Wonders of the World
70	Concert Consternation: Part One
80	Santa's Coming!
82	Dreaming of Christmas
84	Snack Patterns
85	Be Unforgettable!
86	New Year, New You!
87	Finding Inner Strength
88	Did You Know?
89	Christmas Colours
90	Concert Consternation: Part Two
100	Lexa's Guide to Fun and Games
102	Bicycle Brainteaser
103	Find Your Voice
104	Mince Pies
106	The Real You
108	Festive Drinks
110	Answers

Published 2010.
Pedigree Books Ltd, Beech Hill House, Walnut Gardens,
Exeter, Devon EX4 4DH
books@pedigreegroup.co.uk | www.pedigreebooks.com

moxiegirlz.com | mgae.com
TM & © MGA Ent., Inc. U.S. & other countries.
Used under license by Pedigree.

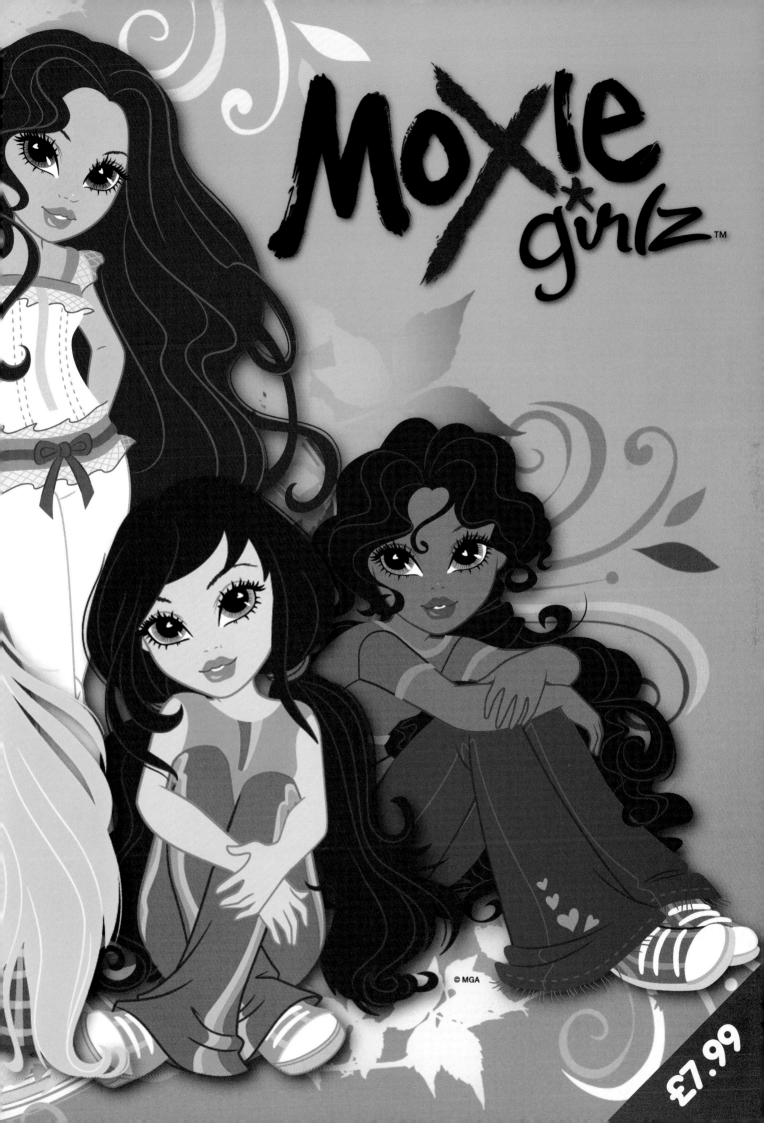

Dear Reader

Welcome to our 2011 Annual! There are lots of fun activities, exciting stories and brilliant games for you to discover. We can't wait for you to start enjoying it!

We've had a mega-exciting year and we're looking forward to finding out what 2011 holds. Let us know about your hopes for the coming year on the page opposite!

We hope that you love our book, and enjoy sharing it with your friends too. And remember, above all else, be true to yourself! Love from

Lexa ×
Sophina ×
Bria ×
Avery ×

Moxie girlz

© MGA

Hopes and Dreams

What will 2011 hold for you?

Use this page to write down all the wonderful things you hope will happen in the coming year, and all your wildest dreams for the future!

Hopes for School...

Hopes for Friends...

Biggest Dream...

© MGA

Lexa
profile

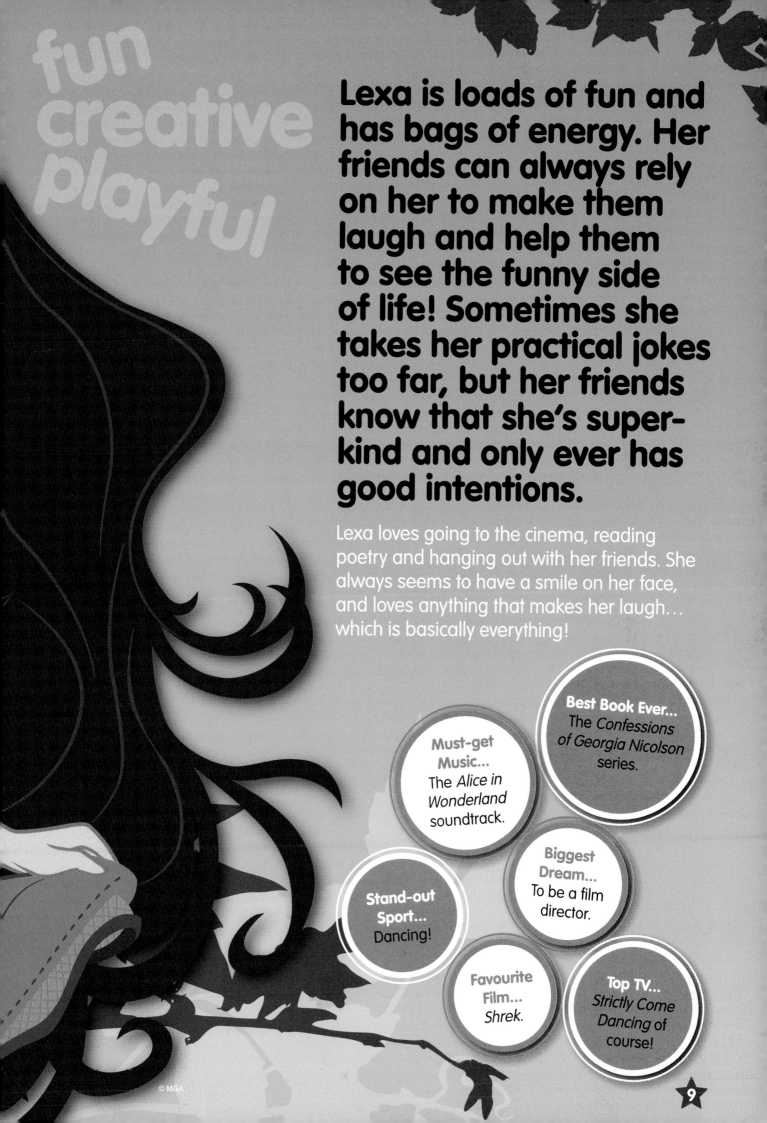

Lexa is loads of fun and has bags of energy. Her friends can always rely on her to make them laugh and help them to see the funny side of life! Sometimes she takes her practical jokes too far, but her friends know that she's super-kind and only ever has good intentions.

Lexa loves going to the cinema, reading poetry and hanging out with her friends. She always seems to have a smile on her face, and loves anything that makes her laugh… which is basically everything!

Best Book Ever...
The *Confessions of Georgia Nicolson* series.

Must-get Music...
The *Alice in Wonderland* soundtrack.

Biggest Dream...
To be a film director.

Stand-out Sport...
Dancing!

Favourite Film...
Shrek.

Top TV...
Strictly Come Dancing of course!

© MGA

9

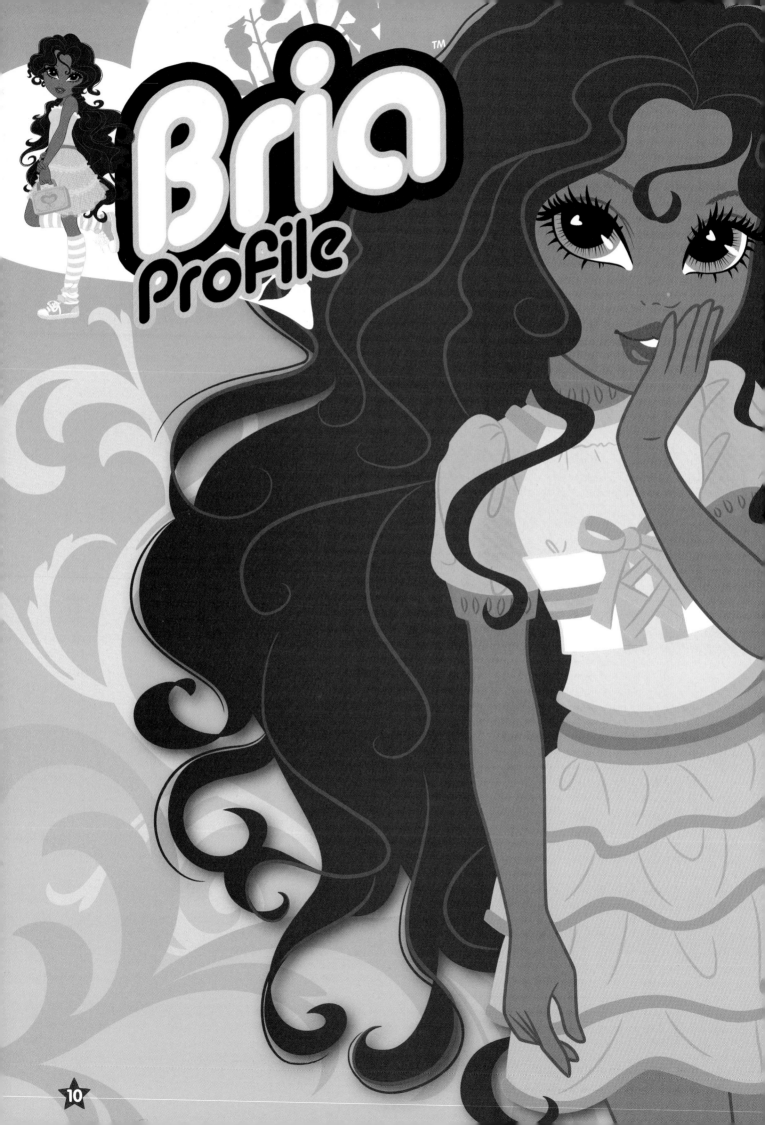

Bria™
Profile

Bria is a talkative, energetic girl with tons of creative ability. She loves sitting in the park people-watching, because she gets so much inspiration from passers-by. Her biggest passion is designing clothes, and she thinks that any item of clothing can be made new again with a bit of imagination.

When Bria's not sketching new fashion designs, she enjoys hanging out with her friends, reading and checking out the latest street fashions!

Best Book Ever... *To Kill A Mockingbird.*

Biggest Dream... To be a fashion designer.

Must-get Music... Japanese pop music.

Stand-out Sport... Snorkelling.

Favourite Film... *Breakfast at Tiffany's.*

Top TV... Fashion channel.

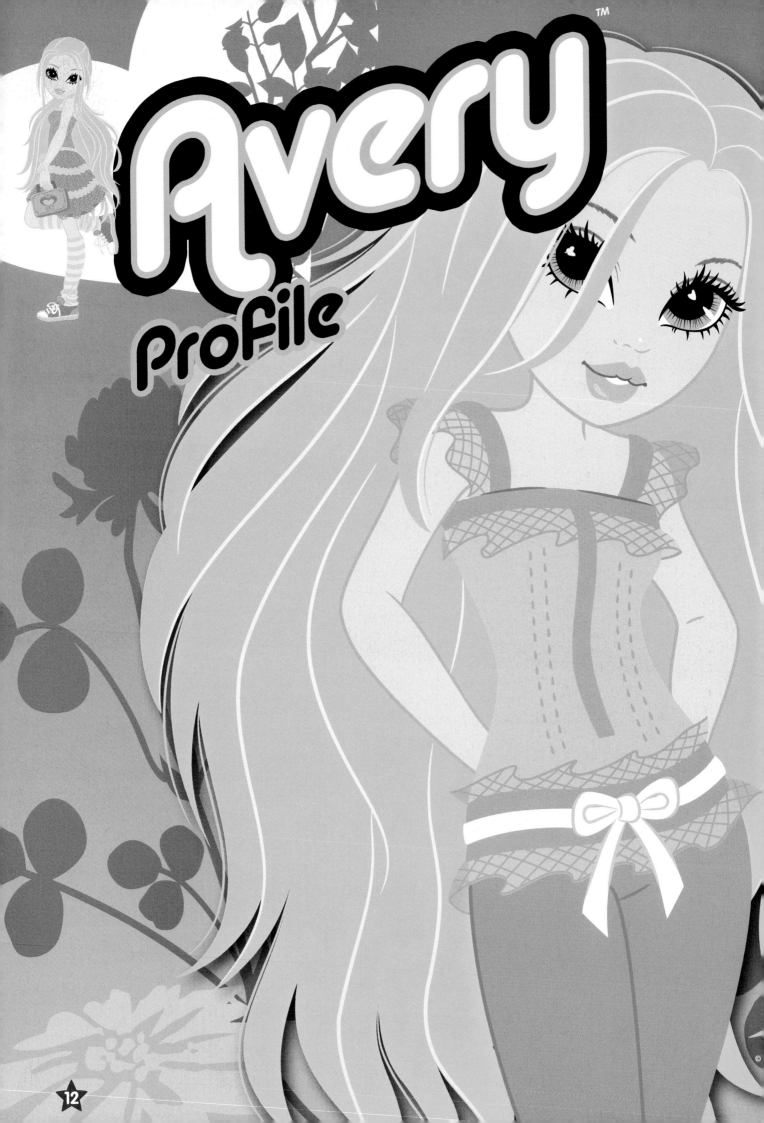

Avery
Profile

strong
determined
energetic

Avery is super-busy because she has huge expectations of herself, and always thinks that she can do anything she puts her mind to. The thing is, she usually can! Avery is determined and ambitious, and makes a great and natural leader. When she's not rock climbing, playing volleyball or catching up with her friends, she's usually updating her blog.

She loves making plans for the future, and that means that sometimes she loses track of the present. Luckily she has her friends to bring her back to reality!

Best Book Ever... Whatever Bria recommends!

Must-get Music... Lady Gaga.

Stand-out Sport... Volleyball.

Favourite Film... *Spiderman.*

Biggest Dream... To be in the Olympics.

Top TV... *Question of Sport.*

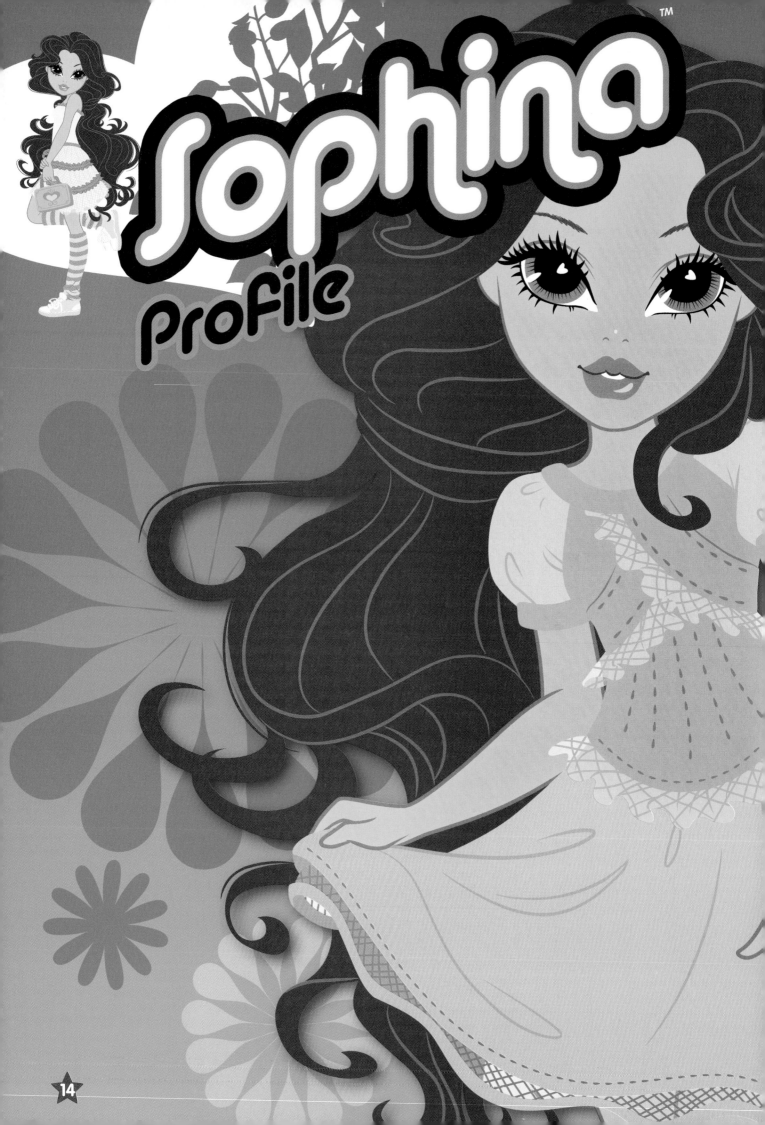

Sophina

profile

warm
thoughtful
caring

Sophina is a true nature girl. She loves animals and everything about the natural world. Her relaxed and thoughtful personality make her a loyal friend. Sophina is quiet, but she has great confidence in her ability to bring about change.

Sophina's idea of a great day out would be a hike through the countryside, followed by dinner over a campfire and a night sleeping under the stars. She spends her spare time writing songs and dreaming of all the fabulous places she's going to travel to when she's older!

Best Book Ever...
Pride and Prejudice.

Must-get Music...
Beyoncé.

Biggest Dream...
To be an environmentalist.

Stand-out Sport...
Hiking in the great outdoors..

Top TV...
I don't watch TV.

Favourite Film...
I love documentaries.

© MGA

All About YOU

© MGA

Now we want to learn all about you! Stick a fabulous photo of yourself in the frame and fill in the blanks!

Stick your picture here

Choose three words that describe you...

Name: Ella

Birthday: 25/12/2000

Home:

Pets: 18

Friends: Holly Lauren Kirsty olivia Alex

My friends say that I'm: good at gum

whisch I am.

I'm most passionate about:

Krindle

kcex

Cronicols
of narnia

Gymnastics

X factor

Jason darulo

tangled

to be in

Olpmpics

Word Creator

How many words can you make from this phrase?
THIS IS GOING TO BE MY YEAR!

Moxie Girlz Magazine

If you were designing a new magazine, what would your first cover look like? What articles would you feature? Whose photos would you include? Use photos, felt tips and pens to create your own magazine cover!

GIRL POWER! Quizzes, puzzles and ....

Moxie girlz™ Magazine

Issue One

Best Friend!
K.HLO

Favourite celeb's

The Friendship Issue

© MGA

I am me!

Use the grid to recreate this fun picture of four friends happily doing their own thing!

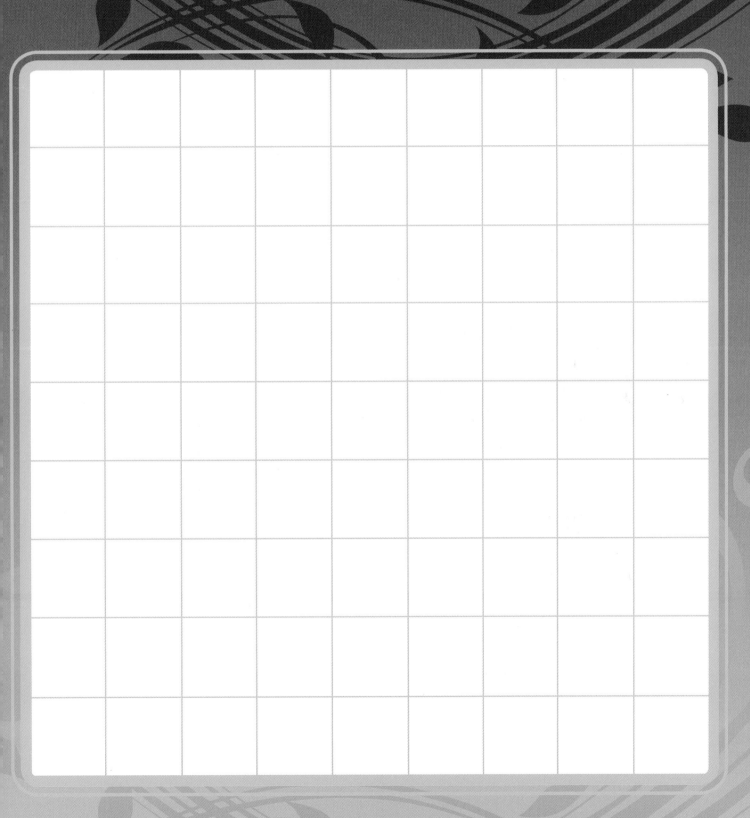

WORLD OF WORDS

Can you find all the hidden country names in this giant wordsearch?

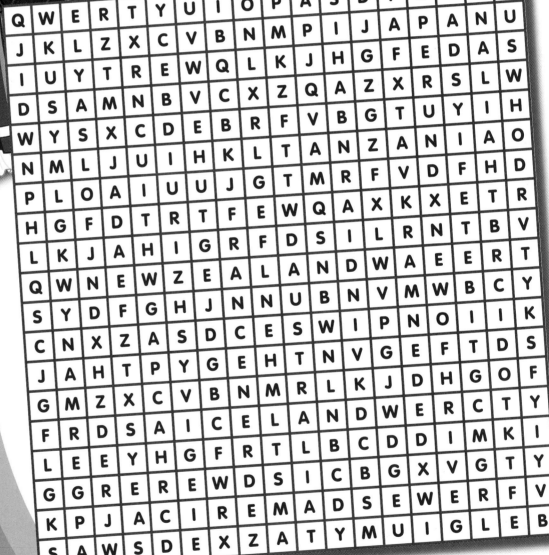

Q	W	E	R	T	Y	U	I	O	P	A	S	D	F	G	H	D	H
J	K	L	Z	X	C	V	B	N	M	P	I	J	A	P	A	N	U
I	U	Y	T	R	E	W	Q	L	K	J	H	G	F	E	D	A	S
D	S	A	M	N	B	V	C	X	Z	Q	A	Z	X	R	S	L	W
W	Y	S	X	C	D	E	B	R	F	V	B	G	T	U	Y	I	H
N	M	L	J	U	I	H	K	L	T	A	N	Z	A	N	I	A	O
P	L	O	A	I	U	U	J	G	T	M	R	F	V	D	F	H	D
H	G	F	D	T	R	T	F	E	W	Q	A	X	K	X	E	T	R
L	K	J	A	H	I	G	R	F	D	S	I	L	R	N	T	B	V
Q	W	N	E	W	Z	E	A	L	A	N	D	W	A	E	E	R	T
S	Y	D	F	G	H	J	N	N	U	B	N	V	M	W	B	C	Y
C	N	X	Z	A	S	D	C	E	S	W	I	P	N	O	I	I	K
J	A	H	T	P	Y	G	E	H	T	N	V	G	E	F	T	D	S
G	M	Z	X	C	V	B	N	M	R	L	K	J	D	H	G	O	F
F	R	D	S	A	I	C	E	L	A	N	D	W	E	R	C	T	Y
L	E	E	Y	H	G	F	R	T	L	B	C	D	D	I	M	K	I
G	G	R	E	R	E	W	D	S	I	C	B	G	X	V	G	T	Y
K	P	J	A	C	I	R	E	M	A	D	S	E	W	E	R	F	V
S	A	W	S	D	E	X	Z	A	T	Y	M	U	I	G	L	E	B

- [ ] AMERICA
- [ ] AUSTRALIA
- [ ] BELGIUM
- [ ] BHUTAN
- [ ] DENMARK
- [ ] EGYPT
- [ ] FRANCE
- [ ] GERMANY
- [ ] GREECE
- [ ] ICELAND
- [ ] INDIA
- [ ] ITALY
- [ ] JAPAN
- [ ] MALAWI
- [ ] MEXICO
- [ ] NEW ZEALAND
- [ ] PERU
- [ ] TANZANIA
- [ ] THAILAND
- [ ] TIBET

22

Spot the Difference

Lexa has been taking photography classes! She's learning to develop her own pictures, but something has gone wrong with these copies. There are ten differences between them – can you spot them all?

© MGA

© MGA

Sophina's Guide
to Amazing Animals

Animals! Big or small, sweet or scary, I love them all! Check out these fast facts about some of my favourite animals on the planet.

© MGA

Great White Shark
These beautiful hunters get really bad press, but when you think about it – they're just doing what comes naturally and being themselves!
Size: Over 6m.
Lifespan: At least thirty years. Some people think they can live for over a hundred years!
Diet: Dolphins, seals, sea lions, porpoises.
Distinguishing features: Large snout, several rows of saw-like teeth.
Unique abilities: Sharks have a special extra sense that allows them to detect the movements of living animals. It can even detect a heartbeat!

Grey Wolf
Wolves are descended from the same ancestors as our pet dogs, but they are much wilder! They totally do their own thing, and that's why I think they are so cool.
Size: Up to 2m long.
Lifespan: Up to ten years in the wild.
Diet: Any meat that's available!
Distinguishing features: Narrow chest, powerful back legs, double-layered coat
Unique abilities: Wolves have special blood vessels in their paws to keep them from freezing.

Elephant

Elephants are the largest land animals on the planet, but they're also super-gentle. They know that size doesn't equal power.

Size: The largest elephant ever recorded was nearly 4m tall!

Lifespan: Between fifty and seventy years.

Diet: Vegetarian.

Distinguishing features: Trunk, tusks, roundish feet.

Unique abilities: Elephants use their ears as a sophisticated cooling system! The network of blood vessels in the large, flapping ears helps to circulate cool blood to the rest of the body.

Meerkat

Meerkats are full of energy and enthusiasm for life, and that's what I love about them!

Size: 25-35cm body length.

Lifespan: Twelve to fourteen years.

Diet: Insects, lizards, eggs, scorpions, spiders.

Distinguishing features: Black patches around the eyes, curved claws for digging and a long tail used for balance.

Unique abilities: Meerkats can close their ears, which helps to keep sand out when they're digging. Each meerkat has a unique pattern of stripes on its back.

Llama

Llamas are friendly and curious, which is a great combination for an interesting life!

Size: Up to 1.8m tall.

Lifespan: Twelve to eighteen years.

Diet: Grass is the staple diet of llamas.

Distinguishing features: Banana-shaped ears, two toes with soft pads, woolly coats.

Unique abilities: Llamas are intelligent animals and are able to learn simple tasks.

Golden Eagle

Golden eagles are beautiful and noble. They're also incredibly loyal – they often mate for life!

Size: Wingspan over 2m.

Lifespan: Over thirty years.

Diet: Rabbits, squirrels, reptiles, fish.

Distinguishing features: Golden feathers around the head and neck.

Unique abilities: Their excellent eyesight, powerful talons and hooked beaks make them extremely efficient hunters.

Tiger

Tigers are amazingly adaptable animals. They can survive in all sorts of different environments. There are lots of stories and poems about them – they have a sort of magic that I completely love!

Size: Up to 3.3m long.

Lifespan: Fifteen to twenty years.

Diet: Meat.

Distinguishing features: Orange-yellow coat, dark brown stripes and a white belly.

Unique abilities: The tiger's roar can be heard almost two miles away!

Animal Challenge

Solve the clues and complete the crossword. When you have finished, rearrange the letters in the shaded squares to discover the name of another amazing animal.

© MGA

Across
1. An eight-legged creature.
4. A friendly sea dweller.
7. A place of learning.
9. To briefly close one eye.
10. A farm animal.

Down
2. An oath.
3. An arc of colours in the sky.
5. A track you can walk on.
6. Something that can keep drinks hot or cold.
8. To raise something up.

Mystery animal:

Odd One Out

Check out these snaps of Bria chatting on the phone. Can you tell which picture is the odd one out?

A.

B.

C.

D.

E.

© MGA © MGA

27

AROUND THE WORLD IN 80 STEPS

Can you be the first to travel around the world? The winner is the first player to return home after globetrotting! You will need a dice, some friends and a counter for each player. And don't forget your passport!

London

Paris

Sydney

1. Roll the dice and work your way around the board.
2. Follow any instructions that you land on.
3. The winner is the first player to reach home.

START

1

You lose your plane ticket. Move back two spaces.

3

You make a new friend on the aeroplane. Swap counter places with the player on your right.

6

The airline lose your bags. Move back one space.

4

8

You send an email home. Move forward two spaces.

You feel homesick. Miss a turn.

11

Mystery Maze

© MGA

"Deighton Hall is so cool," Bria told Sophina, as the school coach bounced them along. "Just wait until you see the maze!"

"And the Grand Hall – that's awesome," Avery added, poking her head over the top of the seats to join in the conversation.

Sophina hadn't been at Riverlake High School for long, but she had already made some great friends. They had helped her to build her confidence, and they had taught her about being a Moxie Girl. Sophina loved their idea that she could make a difference.

Suddenly there were shrieks of laughter from the back seat, where Lexa was juggling with three apples and an orange.

"Lexa, playing with other people's packed lunches is not what I'd call behaving yourself," said the teacher's voice from the front of the coach.

"They don't mind, Mr Hodges," said Lexa.

"Well I do!" he roared. "Stop it now!" There was a horrible silence as everyone turned to look at Lexa. Her cheeks burned with embarrassment as she returned the fruit and went to sit beside Avery. Sophina looked around at her with sympathy.

© MGA

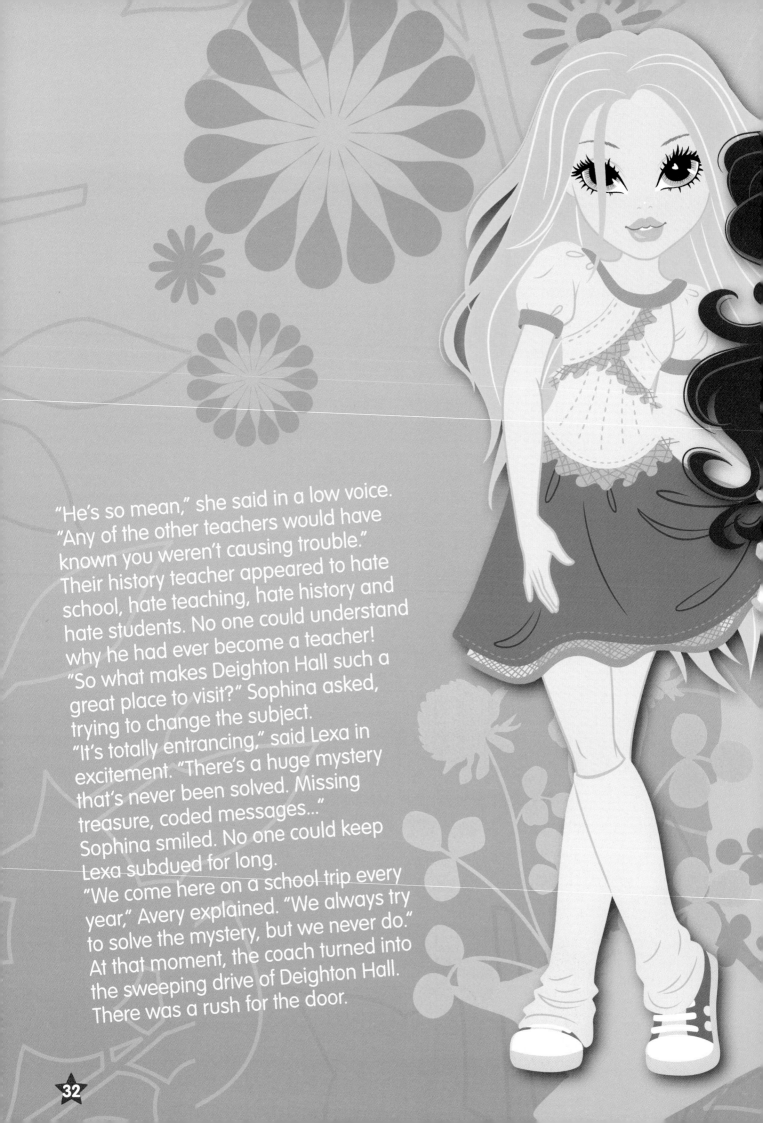

"He's so mean," she said in a low voice. "Any of the other teachers would have known you weren't causing trouble." Their history teacher appeared to hate school, hate teaching, hate history and hate students. No one could understand why he had ever become a teacher!

"So what makes Deighton Hall such a great place to visit?" Sophina asked, trying to change the subject.

"It's totally entrancing," said Lexa in excitement. "There's a huge mystery that's never been solved. Missing treasure, coded messages..."

Sophina smiled. No one could keep Lexa subdued for long.

"We come here on a school trip every year," Avery explained. "We always try to solve the mystery, but we never do."

At that moment, the coach turned into the sweeping drive of Deighton Hall. There was a rush for the door.

"What is the mystery?" asked Sophina, fighting against elbows, bags and shoulders as she tried to get off the coach.
But her friends were lost in the crowd, and by the time she found them again, their guide had met them and was beginning to speak. "Welcome to Deighton Hall!" she said. "My name is Florisa, and I will be showing you around today..."

The tour was a bit boring and Sophina's attention wandered as they walked around the dusty hallways and up spiralling staircases. It was a beautiful old house, but so far she couldn't understand why her friends were so excited about it.

Then, suddenly, they were led into a vast hall that took her breath away. The vaulted ceiling was glittering with chandeliers, and the tall windows dazzled her with the colour of the stained glass. "This is the Grand Hall," said Florisa. "It was in here that the treasure was last seen."

"The treasure?" Sophina asked. "Two hundred years ago, the Deighton family were suspected of having links with pirates," said Florisa. "There was a great robbery at sea and jewels were stolen from a trading ship. A servant reported having seen a massive trunk, full of treasure, in this room. The house and grounds were searched, but the treasure was never discovered. Some people believe that it is still hidden here, somewhere."

"Tell her about the coded message!" Lexa piped up.

"Quiet!" snapped Mr Hodges.

"That's all right," said Florisa with a laugh. "Six weeks ago, a ruined part of the hall was excavated and an exciting note was found. Some people think that it's a clue to where the treasure is hidden."

"Can't you solve it?" asked Avery.

"Not yet," said Florisa with a laugh. "So I'd like you to try. It's on display at the far end of the room."

Sophina and her classmates raced over to the display cases. In the middle of one glass-covered case was a faded, stained piece of paper. Strange words were written on it in shaky, spidery black ink:

Seek your heart's desire beneath the sun.
Look eastwards when the day is halfway done.
In green-walled glory seven steps you'll make.
And underneath amazing treasures take.

Sophina frowned.
"It doesn't make sense," she said.
"If it's a coded message, it's way too vague. Everywhere on the planet is 'beneath the sun'."
Her classmates were drifting away to look at the tapestries hanging on the walls, but Sophina kept staring at the words, reading them over and over again.
"Move along," snapped Mr Hodges behind her.
"Stop dawdling."
"I just thought this was really interesting, sir," said Sophina.
"It must be super-ancient and..."
"Didn't you hear me?" Mr Hodges bellowed.
Sophina hurried after her friends.

© MGA

Lexa put her arm around Sophina's shoulders. "Ignore him," she said. "He's just bad-tempered – as usual. As soon as the tour's finished, let's go and check out the maze. Bria got totally lost in there last time we came!"

"I was not lost!" Bria insisted. "I was just... taking my time."

The girls shouted with laughter and Sophina forgot about the strange rhyme. She only remembered it later that morning when they were outside. There was a big map at the entrance to the maze, showing the correct way through. Sophina's eyes were drawn to a large circle in the top right-hand corner.

"What's that?" she asked, pointing at it.
"It's a massive sundial type thing," Avery replied.
"It's sunk into the ground – you can walk on it. But it tells you the time just like a normal sundial."
The rhyme crashed back into Sophina's mind and she clutched her friends' arms.
"Seek your heart's desire beneath the sun!" she said.
Avery, Bria and Lexa exchanged glances.
"That's it," said Lexa. "She's gone loopy. She's finally cracked."
"It's the rhyme!" Sophina exclaimed, her heart thumping. "The message! The code! Don't you get it? The treasure must be buried under the sundial!"

Continued on page 50

© MGA

COLOUR COUNT

We love these cool shapes and bright colours. How many of each picture can you count? Fill in the boxes and then check your answers to find out how eagle-eyed you really are!

© MGA

40

SWEET SUDOKU

Check out this super-challenging Sudoku square. It's so tough that we think it'll require all your logic skills to solve it. Set a timer and record how long it takes you to complete the puzzle!

Remember, each row and column must include numbers 1 to 9 in any order. Also, each small 3 by 3 square must include numbers 1 to 9.

Style Yourself!

© MGA

Why pay out for a bracelet that anyone can own, when you can make a totally unique piece of jewellery for yourself?

Follow these step-by-step instructions to create an eye-popping bracelet. It's all about expressing your artitude!

You will need:
Embroidery thread in four different colours.
Scissors.
Masking tape.

1. Cut four lengths of embroidery thread, one in each colour. Each piece should be 70cm long.

2. Tie the four threads together with a knot. Leave 6cm of thread spare above the knot.

3. With a piece of masking tape over the knot, hold the threads down on a table.

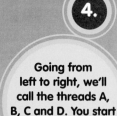

4. Going from left to right, we'll call the threads A, B, C and D. You start with thread A on the far left.

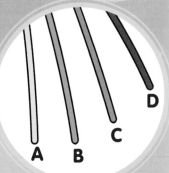

A B C D

5.

Loop thread A over and under thread B.

6.

Hold thread B firmly and pull the knot tight. Repeat this so you have a double knot.

7.

Loop thread A around threads C and D in the same way.

8.

Now you should find that thread A is on the far right and thread B is on the far left.

9.

Now you start again at step 5. Loop thread B over and under the other threads in the same way as before, tying double knots around each of the other strings from left to right.

10.

Keep repeating steps 5–8 until the bracelet is long enough to go around your friend's wrist.

11.

Tie the threads off with a knot, leaving about 6cm of thread at the end.

12.

Use the two ends of the bracelet to tie it around your best friend's wrist!

© MGA

43

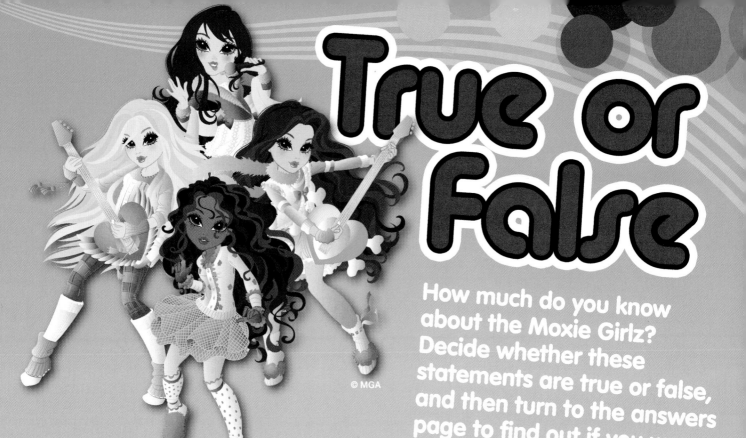

True or False

How much do you know about the Moxie Girlz? Decide whether these statements are true or false, and then turn to the answers page to find out if you were correct. Good luck!

© MGA

1. Avery can be a bit lazy sometimes.
2. Bria is extremely artistic.
3. Lexa dreams of being a film director.
4. Avery is bored by sport.
5. Bria doesn't like competitive sports.
6. Lexa loves to dance.
7. Bria isn't interested in fashion.
8. Bria dislikes the ocean.
9. Lexa never plays practical jokes.
10. Sophina cares about the environment.
11. Sophina is not scared of spiders.
12. Sophina doesn't enjoy TV.
13. Avery plays volleyball.
14. Sophina enjoys hiking.
15. Lexa is a serious girl.

True	False
True	False
True	False
True	False
True	False
True	False
True	False
True	False
True	False
True	False
True	False
True	False
True	False
True	False
True	False

Avery's Amazing Adventure

Avery is on a school trip to a famous mansion, but she got lost in the vast gardens of the stately home.

To find her teacher and her classmates, she has to find her way through this maze. Can you help her out?

Start

Finish

Bria's Guide to Travel

There are so many awesome places in the world, and I never get tired of discovering them. Here's my guide to my all-time favourite destinations – how many of them have you visited already?

© MGA

Florence, Italy
Florence is one of the most beautiful cities in the world. I totally fell in love with it the first day I was there! It's full of winding streets, open piazzas, great food and incredible art.

Don't Miss
The Duomo / The Accademia Museum / The Ponte Vecchio
The markets selling fabulous Italian clothes!

Heidelberg, Germany
This small, friendly city is one of my favourite places in Germany. It's got a really happy vibe, and there is something super romantic about it too!

Don't Miss
Heidelberg Castle / Philosopher's Walk

Paris, France
When you visit Paris, the first place you should check out is the Eiffel Tower. It's a work of art in itself! When you've climbed the steps and seen the incredible view over Paris, head for the Louvre Museum and take a look at the Mona Lisa.

There is so much to do and see in Paris that I can't even begin to name everything! But make sure you take the time to sit on the bank of the River Seine and enjoy some delicious cheese with a rustic baguette!

Don't Miss
Sacré Coeur / Tuileries Gardens / A trip down the river in a tour boat / Notre Dame Cathedral

Jaipur, India

A city of colour, sound and wonder, this is one place not to miss. Camels use the roads alongside cars and vans! For unforgettable entertainment, plan a trip to the cinema. It's unlike anything you will have experienced at home!

Jaipur brims over with energy. The shops nestle closely together selling silks and satins, bags of bright spices and exquisite jewellery, while the marketplaces are filled with enticing clothes and materials. I loved every moment of my trip!

Don't Miss
Jantar Mantar / The Palace quarter / Amber Fort / The Albert Hall Museum

Copenhagen, Denmark

The capital city of Denmark is a major centre of culture. The people who live there have great quality of life, and it's one of the most environmentally friendly cities in the world.

Hire a bicycle if you want to see the city like a local! There are beaches within cycling distance, loads of parks and tons of cool places to visit.

Don't Miss
The Marble Church / The Pantomime Theatre / Rosenborg Castle
The statue of the Little Mermaid

The South Island, New Zealand

The South Island is incredibly beautiful, and it's a great place to do some exploring by hiking and camping. The landscape here will take your breath away – it's like the setting for an epic fantasy story! There are high mountains, rugged coastlines and glittering glaciers. Don't forget to take your camera!

Don't Miss
Marlborough Sounds / Lake Wanaka / Queenstown Southern Lakes

New York City, America

The Statue of Liberty is an icon of New York City and of America itself. Don't miss out on a chance to visit it. But when you have ticked that off your list, make some time to look around the rest of the city too. You might have seen a lot of it in films and TV shows already, but nothing can prepare you for the buzz, glamour and energy of the real thing!

Don't Miss
Times Square / Chrysler Building / Empire State Building / Central Park

Rome, Italy

Rome is famous for its imposing Colosseum. But there is more to Rome than one well-known monument! Make your way to the heart of the city and visit the Sistine Chapel. Check out the impressive Pantheon and the ancient Catacombs. It's a fabulous city, bursting with life, culture and drama.

Don't Miss
Sistine Chapel / St Peter's Basilica / The Pantheon / The Catacombs

I love sharing the places I'm passionate about with my friends.
What's your favourite place and why?

Design of Dreams

What would your bedroom look like if you could have anything in the world? Let your imagination soar and use this space to design the bedroom of your dreams. Think about what furniture, materials and colours you would use. Start with a pencil sketch, and then use your felt tips to complete the design. There are some ideas scattered around the page to inspire you!

Curtains

Dressing table

Sleek lines

Cushions

Four-poster bed

Water bed

French windows

Chandeliers

Bold colours

Canopy

Beanbags

Elegance

Silk

Rugs

Gold brocade

Wardrobe

Muddle and Match

We've been ice-skating with friends, but someone has made a big mess in the changing room. All our shoes and boots are muddled up!

Can you help us to put the right shoes and boots together? Draw lines to match up the pairs.

© MGA

49

Mystery Maze Part Two

"So – what now?" asked Bria. Everyone looked at Sophina. They were standing around the large, flat sundial in the depths of the maze. Sophina didn't reply. She looked down at the sundial and then stared off into the distance.

"We can't dig under the sundial," said Avery. "Even if the treasure is buried there, it would take diggers and proper machinery."
"I was wrong," said Sophina slowly. "There's more to it than just the sundial."
"I still think she's gone loopy," said Lexa with a laugh.
"What do you mean, Sophina?" Bria asked.

"Think about it," said Sophina. "The first line of the rhyme says 'Seek your heart's desire beneath the sun.' If we assume that the 'heart's desire' is the treasure and 'the sun' is the sundial, then we're in the right place, agreed?"
"Agreed," said her friends together.
"But there's more to the rhyme," said Sophina.
She stood in the centre of the sundial and recited:

"Look eastwards when the day is halfway done.
In green-walled glory seven steps you'll make.
And underneath amazing treasures take."

"So... we have to look eastwards?" said Avery.
"Yes," said Sophina, "but only 'when the day is halfway done.'"
"That must mean twelve o'clock," said Lexa.
"It's two minutes to twelve now!" exclaimed Avery in excitement. "Oh wow! We are going to solve the mystery and find the treasure and be in all the newspapers and..."
"Hang on, we have to solve the message first!" said Bria with a laugh.

The points of the compass were engraved into the stone sundial. The girls turned to face east and Lexa began a countdown to midday.

"Twenty-one... twenty... nineteen..."

"But what are we even looking for?" asked Bria in a whisper.

"Fifteen... fourteen... thirteen..."

"I don't know," said Sophina. "The rhyme says 'green-walled glory'..."

"Seven... six... five..."

"But we're surrounded by 'green walls'," said Avery, staring at the green hedges of the maze. "How are we supposed to know which one it means?"

"It's time!" said Lexa.

Sophina glimpsed something shining in the hedge in front of her. It was reflecting the light of the sun.

"Look!" she exclaimed. "What is that?"

It looked like a pole sticking straight out of the middle of the hedge. At the very top of it, something was gleaming.

"It's a piece of glass, or a mirror or something," said Bria.

"It's set into the pole," Avery realised. "It must be angled so that the sun shines on it at midday."

"But what does it mean?" Lexa asked. "What are we supposed to do now?"

"'In green-walled glory seven steps you'll take'," repeated Sophina. "I think we have to take seven steps from the pole, right through the middle of the hedge."

"And underneath amazing treasures take," Bria finished.

"Oh – amazing treasures! We have to dig under the maze!"

"Seven steps from the pole," said Sophina, feeling dizzy with excitement. "Come on!"

She ran to the hedge and pushed her head and shoulders through the thick green leaves. It was hard to see anything, and tiny branches scratched her face.

"I have to get further in," she called to the others.

Bria and Avery pulled the sides of the hedge around her, and then Lexa gave her one enormous shove. With a squeal, Sophina toppled into the middle of the hedge.

"Are you okay?" called Bria's voice.

"Fine!" Sophina replied. "It's hollow inside."

She scrambled over to the base of the pole. It looked very old. She began counting seven steps away from it. Suddenly there was a rustling and her friends' heads poked through the bush.

"Well?" Lexa demanded.

"What can you see?" asked Avery.

"Seven!" said Sophina.

She scraped away at the soil and then gave an exclamation.

"What is it?" Bria squealed.

"There's a sort of metal ring stuck in the ground, under the soil," said Sophina in a thrilled whisper.

But before she could discover more, the girls got a terrible shock

"What is going on here?" bellowed a voice.

It was Mr Hodges!

Five minutes later, all four girls were being frogmarched to the Director of Visits' office. It didn't matter how hard they tried to explain what they had been doing; Mr Hodges wouldn't listen.

Mr Hodges strode into the Director's office. The girls could hear him explaining what they had done.

"They're wilful, naughty liars who love causing trouble," he said.

"That's not true!" cried Lexa, bursting in to the room. The others followed her, and the Director stared at them in astonishment.

"Get out!" shouted Mr Hodges.

"No," said the Director. "I believe in hearing all sides of a story. Girls, can you explain yourselves?"

Sophina stepped forward. She felt indignant and upset that Mr Hodges didn't believe them, but she spoke calmly.

"We're not liars," she said. "Our tour guide, Florisa, showed us the rhyming message and said that we should try to work out what it meant. That's exactly what we did."

Mr Hodges gave a disbelieving snort, but Sophina ignored him. She told the Director how they had suspected that the sundial had something to do with the rhyme. She explained how they had seen the pole hidden in the hedge, and how she had clambered inside to walk the seven steps.

When she came to the part about the metal ring in the ground, the Director's eyes lit up.

"I've never heard of that before!" he said.

He started making excitable phone calls and the four friends stared at each other in delight. Could they really have found the treasure?

The next day, at school, the girls were called to see the head teacher. He gave them a beaming smile. "I have some good news," he said. "After your visit to Deighton Hall yesterday, an area of the maze was dug up, and a secret underground chamber was found."

"Oh!" gasped Sophina. "Was the treasure there?"

"There was a large trunk there," said the head teacher. "And inside the trunk were jewels that have been missing for over two hundred years!"

"We did it!" said Avery, hardly able to believe her ears. "We actually did it!"

"The Director of Visits is going to donate some money to the school as a thank you," said the head teacher. "And the local newspapers want to interview you all!"

Dizzy with excitement, the girls left the head teacher's office and walked slowly back to their classroom. Up ahead, they saw Mr Hodges. He scowled at them and scurried away. "That'll teach him not to listen to students' ideas!" said Lexa with a laugh.

"You know what," said Sophina, "I think it was Moxie that found that treasure – it was the power of positive thinking!"

The four of them linked arms.

"You're right," said Avery. "Moxie means having the power to do anything – even treasure hunting!"

The End

© MGA

59

PERFECTION PLANNER

Everyone has an idea of their perfect day with friends. We want you to plan yours!

Fill out the sections on these pages to dream up your ideal day out.

© MGA

Meeting Place

Meeting Time

Who's Invited?

Dress Code

Food

Organiser _____

Number of vegetarians _____

Any likes/dislikes/allergies _____

Menu plan _____

Drinks

Organiser _____

Any likes/dislikes/allergies _____

Menu plan _____

Drinks

Organiser _____

Any likes/dislikes/allergies _____

Menu plan _____

Transport _____

_____

_____

Activities _____

_____

Photographer _____

_____

**Any Other
Necessities**
(e.g. map, shopping
bags, bikes)
_____

_____

Schedule
10am-11am
11am-12pm
12pm-1pm
1pm-2pm
2pm-3pm
3pm-4pm

Devastating Detective Skills

Play this observational game to find out if your detective skills are up to scratch. First, set a timer for one minute. In those sixty seconds, stare at the pictures on this page and try to memorise as many of them as you can. As soon as the timer goes off, cover this page with a piece of paper and answer the questions on the page opposite.

© MGA

Answer as many of these questions as you can. You get one point for each correct answer.

1. How is Lexa wearing her hair?

2. What colour are Sophina's braces?

3. What colour is the cupcake?

4. Which girl is wearing a red outfit?

5. What food item in the picture is black?

6. What colour is Lexa's book?

7. How many strings are on the guitar?

8. Which girl is wearing long boots?

9. What colour is the paintbrush?

10. Who has hearts printed on her top?

Bonus Question
For an extra five points, who is standing with her hands on her hips?

0-7
Oh dear, your memory needs a bit more exercise before you can be a detective!

8-12
Not bad, but you should play the memory game every day to really sharpen your detective skills.

13-14
Wow, you're a born detective!

Japanese Inspiration

Sophina has been totally inspired by this awesome art style from Japan!

She's designed a super-cool outfit for herself, but she needs your help to complete three more outfits for her friends. Grab your boldest colours and your wildest design ideas, and go for it. Then design an eye-popping outfit for yourself!

© MGA

Design your outfit here:

We love this big picture of us singing and dancing, but it needs colour to really bring it to life! Use your felt tips or colouring pencils to complete the portrait.

© MGA

Avery's Wonders of the World

The world is full of awesome sights and incredible places. I wish I could visit them all! But this is my all-time favourites list – what's yours?

© MGA

The Taj Mahal, India

This breathtaking monument was built by an emperor to honour the memory of his wife. It is one of the most beautiful buildings in the world, and it sits on the banks of the River Yamuna.

Out of respect, visitors must take off their shoes. You will feel the cool marble beneath your feet and the breeze from the river on your face. Sure, you can look at pictures of it, but nothing can prepare you for the real thing. The fact that it's linked to a love story just makes it all the more magical!

The Egyptian Pyramids, Egypt

The Pyramids of Giza were once one of the Seven Wonders of the World. They were built thousands of years ago, as burial chambers for kings. Corridors descend into the pyramids, leading to galleries and chambers that were once filled with treasure.

Visit the Great Sphinx, which has the face of a man and the body of a lion, and rest your hands on the limestone. It is amazing to think of how long it has stood there and how many people have put their hands on the same spot over the centuries.

Niagara Falls, America

This cataract is one of the most spectacular sights in the world. The water is so clear and beautiful as it flows over the falls. It looks like giant, glassy curtains! Behind the water is the Cave of the Winds, and you can also view the falls from Rainbow Bridge. How cool are those names!

Machu Picchu, Peru

The ancient Inca city of Machu Picchu is perched high above a valley between two sharp peaks. It is a staggering sight, when you think about the skill and effort that must have gone into building it hundreds of years ago.

You can trek through the mountains on foot to reach Machu Picchu at daybreak. The Inca people used to worship the sun. When you stand in the ruins of this magnificent city and watch the sun rising over the mountain peaks, perhaps you will understand why!

The Colosseum, Italy

The Colosseum in Rome was built about 70 AD, and it was used as a stage for what the Romans called 'games'. They held hand-to-hand fights between fearsome gladiators here, as well as contests between animals and men. Over the centuries it has been used for many different purposes. At one time, people even lived within its walls!

When I walked around the structure and listened to the guide talking about its history, I got a really strong sense of being surrounded by shadows of the past. Creepy – but cool!

Grand Canyon, America

This vast canyon was formed by the Colorado River cutting through the high plateaus of Arizona. Its size and colour is awe-inspiring, with reds, greys, pinks and violets making it look like a work of art. It's dizzying in its size, and it's definitely not the place to visit if you're scared of heights! But I fell in love with this beautiful place.

Table Mountain, South Africa

This flat-topped mountain overlooks Cape Town, and its peculiar shape brings visitors from all over the world. It is formed by horizontal layers of sandstone. Even though the face of the mountain is harsh and stark, the top is green and lush, with streams and valleys.

Up on Table Mountain you might see orchids, silver trees, and even goats. The views are fantastic, and standing up there made me feel as if I had found the top of the world!

Concert Consternation

Part One

"Snow," said Sophina, staring out of the sitting room window. "I thought I wanted it to snow this Christmas, but not if it spoils the concert!"

"I'm afraid it sounds as if it will," said her mum, walking into the room. "That was the last of the school drama clubs on the phone. Because of the snow, they can't get here in time for the concert."

Sophina groaned and flopped back onto the sofa. Her mum was the secretary of the Riverlake Amateur Dramatic Society, and they had spent weeks organising a big Christmas concert for charity. All the schools in the local area had signed up to join in, and everyone had been looking forward to it. Now the snow was going to spoil everything.

"There's only one thing to do," said Sophina's mum. "We'll have to cancel the concert."

"Oh no!' cried Sophina. "Mum, there must be something we can do?"

"Sophina, every school was doing an act," said her mum with a sigh. "Now that the roads are blocked with snow, the only school that can perform is Riverlake High, which means we only have two acts. It's not enough. We'll simply have to refund the tickets."

"But that means all the children won't get Christmas presents," Sophina said, feeling miserable. The money from the concert was being donated to a charity that sent Christmas presents to children in deprived areas. Sophina and her friends had been very excited to help. It was going to be their job to work backstage and make sure everything ran smoothly.

"I'd better phone the others," said Sophina. "They're going to be so disappointed."

The first person she called was Lexa. She explained that the snow was stopping people from getting to Riverlake.

"Mum's going to have to refund the tickets on the door," she said.

"Nonsense," said Lexa briskly.

"Pardon?" said Sophina in surprise.

"I'm not letting a bit of snow stop my fun!" said Lexa with a laugh.

"But we've only got two acts for the show," Sophina reminded her.

"Then we'll just have to find some more," said Lexa. "I'll round up the others and we'll head over to your house straight away."

"Are you sure about this?" asked Sophina.

"We're Moxie Girlz, remember?" Lexa exclaimed. "We can do anything!"

Half an hour later there was a knock on the door. Bria, Avery and Lexa were standing there in thick coats, hats and wellies. They were covered in snow, but they were rosy cheeked and laughing.

"Concert Rescue Team reporting for duty!" said Lexa. "Let us in, Sophina – it's freezing out here!"

Sophina's mum made hot chocolate with marshmallows for everyone as the snow continued to fall outside. "We have a violin recital and a magic act," Sophina said. "That's not enough for a concert."
"There are loads of people in Riverlake with talent," said Bria. "I bet we can get some of them to help us out. After all, it's for a good cause."

"Let's make a list," Avery suggested. "And I think the first name on it should be Lexa."
"What?" squeaked Lexa. "What can I do?"
"Are you kidding?" said Bria. "You're the funniest person I know! You can do a comedy routine – you'll have everyone crying with laughter."
A little grin started to appear on Lexa's face and her eyes sparkled. "I have thought up some cool new jokes recently," she said. "I could try them out..."

© MGA

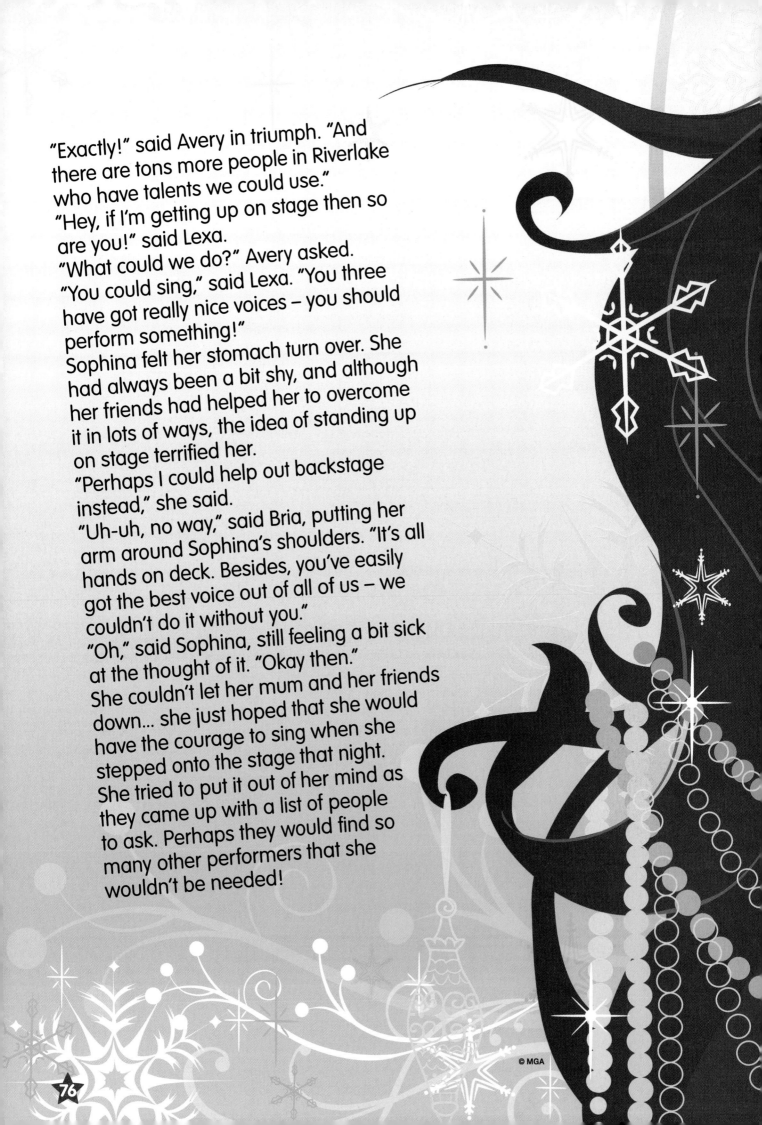

"Exactly!" said Avery in triumph. "And there are tons more people in Riverlake who have talents we could use."

"Hey, if I'm getting up on stage then so are you!" said Lexa.

"What could we do?" Avery asked.

"You could sing," said Lexa. "You three have got really nice voices – you should perform something!"

Sophina felt her stomach turn over. She had always been a bit shy, and although her friends had helped her to overcome it in lots of ways, the idea of standing up on stage terrified her.

"Perhaps I could help out backstage instead," she said.

"Uh-uh, no way," said Bria, putting her arm around Sophina's shoulders. "It's all hands on deck. Besides, you've easily got the best voice out of all of us – we couldn't do it without you."

"Oh," said Sophina, still feeling a bit sick at the thought of it. "Okay then."

She couldn't let her mum and her friends down... she just hoped that she would have the courage to sing when she stepped onto the stage that night. She tried to put it out of her mind as they came up with a list of people to ask. Perhaps they would find so many other performers that she wouldn't be needed!

The girls thought of everyone they knew. Anyone who had a talent was added to the list. School friends, teachers and neighbours were all considered. At last they had a long list of potential performers. Now they just had to persuade them to say yes!

"Let's divide the list between us," Bria suggested. "We can each take a few names. That will be much quicker."

They pulled on their warm coats, wellies and hats again, and wrapped thick scarves around their necks. "Good luck," said Sophina's mum. "I really hope that you girls can make this concert happen."

"I totally believe we can," said Avery with confidence. "Come on, let's go!"

They left the house and tramped through the snow to the end of the street. Snow whirled and eddied around them. Sophina could feel the tip of her nose getting colder and colder. When they reached the end of the street, Avery turned to face them. "This is where we separate," she said. "Let's meet back at Sophina's house as soon as we've seen everyone on our lists. Good luck, everyone!"

Continued on page 90

Santa's Coming!

Follow these simple instructions to create our funky Santa tree decorations!

You will need:
Red, pink, black and brown felt. Needle and red thread. Red ribbon. Fabric glue. Pair of wiggly eyes. Cotton wool. Scissors

1. Cut two Santa body shapes from red felt, using the template to help you.

2. Cut a length of ribbon and put the ends between the two felt bodies. (The ribbon will hang from the top of the head, and you can use it to hang the decoration on your tree.)

3. Cut two boot shapes from black felt. Place them between the two bodies so they stick out from the bottom of the Santa figure.

4. Ask an adult to help you sew the bodies together, holding the ribbon and boots in place. Leave a small gap, which you will use to stuff the decoration.

5. Fill the Santa with cotton wool and then sew the gap closed.

6. For Santa's face, cut out a pink circle of felt and glue it to the body. Glue on the eyes and add some cotton wool for the beard.

7. For Santa's belt, cut a long, thin rectangular shape from brown felt and glue it onto the body.

Santa's body

Santa's face

Santa's belt

Santa's boots

Dreaming of Christmas

Roasting marshmallows over a fire or enjoying a barbeque on the beach – what would make your perfect Christmas? Complete this quiz and find out.

1. What's your favourite season of the year?
a. Summer
b. Winter
c. Spring
d. Autumn

2. If you could time travel anywhere, where would you choose?
a. One hundred years in the future.
b. Victorian Britain.
c. The 1980s.
d. The 1920s.

3. What do you enjoy watching on television?
a. Big feature films.
b. Reality TV shows.
c. Intelligent comedies.
d. Classic movies.

4. Where do you feel most relaxed?
a. On holiday.
b. At home.
c. Enjoying the bright lights of the city.
d. On long walks in the countryside.

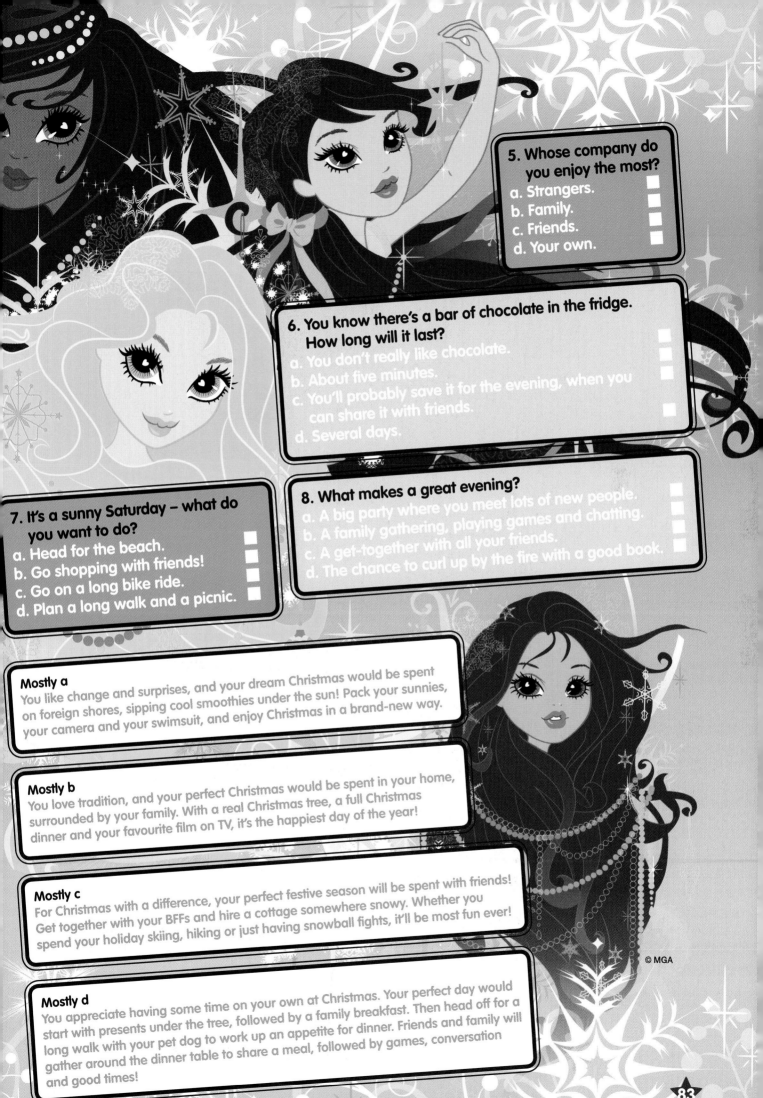

5. Whose company do you enjoy the most?
a. Strangers.
b. Family.
c. Friends.
d. Your own.

6. You know there's a bar of chocolate in the fridge. How long will it last?
a. You don't really like chocolate.
b. About five minutes.
c. You'll probably save it for the evening, when you can share it with friends.
d. Several days.

7. It's a sunny Saturday – what do you want to do?
a. Head for the beach.
b. Go shopping with friends!
c. Go on a long bike ride.
d. Plan a long walk and a picnic.

8. What makes a great evening?
a. A big party where you meet lots of new people.
b. A family gathering, playing games and chatting.
c. A get-together with all your friends.
d. The chance to curl up by the fire with a good book.

Mostly a
You like change and surprises, and your dream Christmas would be spent on foreign shores, sipping cool smoothies under the sun! Pack your sunnies, your camera and your swimsuit, and enjoy Christmas in a brand-new way.

Mostly b
You love tradition, and your perfect Christmas would be spent in your home, surrounded by your family. With a real Christmas tree, a full Christmas dinner and your favourite film on TV, it's the happiest day of the year!

Mostly c
For Christmas with a difference, your perfect festive season will be spent with friends! Get together with your BFFs and hire a cottage somewhere snowy. Whether you spend your holiday skiing, hiking or just having snowball fights, it'll be most fun ever!

Mostly d
You appreciate having some time on your own at Christmas. Your perfect day would start with presents under the tree, followed by a family breakfast. Then head off for a long walk with your pet dog to work up an appetite for dinner. Friends and family will gather around the dinner table to share a meal, followed by games, conversation and good times!

SNACK patterns

Look at these unfinished patterns. Can you figure out how they should continue, and complete them all? Use your colouring pencils to finish the patterns.

Be unforgettable!

Every Moxie Girl knows that she has the power to change the world. But how do you go about making yourself unforgettable? It's all about how you feel about yourself and how you treat other people. Check out our tips and be extraordinary!

Treat other people as you would like them to treat you.

Do something for another person every day.

Look for things to like about other people.

Be honest.

What do you like best about yourself? Remind yourself of one thing every morning.

Join a club or a group.

Is there an issue or cause that you feel strongly about? Whatever your passion is, get involved and start making a difference.

Always look for the bright side of a situation.

Set yourself a project to raise money for your favourite charity.

Do some exercise every week.

Listen to your friends. Good listeners are great friends.

Write down your goals and wishes, and always have them in mind.

Look out for opportunities.

Don't get involved in gossip.

Laugh! It's the best medicine, so learn a few jokes and get your friends giggling too.

LOVE · STRONG · SMART

© MGA

New Year, New You!

What are your predictions and resolutions for 2011?

Think about your expectations for the coming year, and then fill out the sections on this page.

My Top Ten Predictions for 2011

1.
2.
3.
4.
5.
6.
7.
8.
9.
10.

© MGA

My New Year's Resolutions for 2011

What will you be doing on this day a year from now?

What would you like to improve about yourself in 2011?

Finding Inner Strength

Being a Moxie Girl is all about finding your own inner strength and focus.

But sometimes, in the whirl of friends, family and school, that can be difficult. We put our heads together and came up with a few tips to give you a helping hand.

Keep Calm
When you are angry or upset, you cannot behave rationally.

Do It Your Way
Experiment with different calming methods. Perhaps meditation will work for you, or maybe dancing is the key to shaking off your negative emotions.

Learn from the Past
Think about times in the past when you have made it through tough times. This will show you that you have inner strength.

Get Perspective
If you're in the middle of a difficult situation, ask yourself some questions to figure out how important it really is.
Will this matter tomorrow?
Will it matter in a week?
Will it matter in a month?
Will it matter in a year?
Does this experience define your life or who you are?

Learn
Building your knowledge will help you to achieve your dreams.

Believe in Yourself
Remind yourself every day of all the good things about yourself. You are entitled to live your dreams!

Make Plans
Your life is an exciting journey, and you can decide on its direction. Making plans is fun and important, even if they change and develop along the way.

Join a Group
Do you have an interest that you could share with others? Consider getting involved in a group such as a sports club, photography association or writing circle.

Celebrate
Be glad about achieving your goals.

Have Patience
Never stop trying and believing that your dreams will come true.

Keep it Simple
Simplicity is the key to straightforward friendships, honest living and uncomplicated happiness!

Be Honest
Show affection for other people – don't bottle it all up inside. Letting your friends know that you care makes them feel supported, safe and happy.

© MGA

87

Did You Know?

We love Christmas time! Check out these fascinating facts about the festive season.

- Boxing Day gets its name from the charity boxes that used to be placed outside churches over Christmas. On December 26 the boxes would be opened and the contents would be shared among the poor.

- It used to be believed throughout Europe that on Christmas Eve, farmyard animals everywhere knelt down and spoke in human voices.

- People have decorated their houses with evergreens at Christmas time as far back as Druid times. Holly, ivy and mistletoe were supposed to be magical plants.

- The tradition of decorated Christmas trees came from Germany with Prince Albert. In those days, the trees were decorated with gilded fruits and nuts, sweets, paper roses and miniature candles.

- Santa Claus has many names around the world. He is known as Father Christmas in the UK, Kriss Kringle in Germany and Julinesse in Denmark.

- The first Christmas card was designed in 1843.

- A Christmas wreath hanging on your front door is meant to symbolise welcome and long life for all guests.

- According to tradition, you should eat mince pies in silence and make a wish with each one.

- An old Christmas myth says that if you bake bread on Christmas Eve, it will never go mouldy.

Make the most of your holiday!

© MGA

Christmas Colours

It's Christmas time and there's a big party, but we need some stunning new outfits for the occasion. Use your colouring pens and pencils to create four unique styles. Complete the outfits by gluing on glitter, beads or feathers.

© MGA

Concert Consternation Part Two

Sophina rushed to see the first person on her list – or rather the first people on her list.

"We need your help!" she gasped, when the Connor twins came to their front door.

Adam and Liam Connor were in Sophina's class at school. They were always mucking around in class, making fun of the girls and talking about music when they should have been working. But right now, Sophina was really pleased that they liked music so much!

"You want to be in a band, right?" she asked.

"Yes, why?" asked Liam.

"Because tonight's your chance," said Sophina. "The roads are blocked, and the concert's going to be cancelled unless we can find some new acts. Will you play some of your songs?"

"What's in it for us?" asked Adam. Sophina frowned at him.
"You mean, apart from the chance to give Christmas presents to children living in poverty?" she asked.

"Er..." said Adam, staring at his feet.
"Count us in," said Liam, rolling his eyes at his brother.
"Brilliant!" exclaimed Sophina. She told them to grab their guitars and head over to the town hall to practise. Then she set off to see the next person on her list.

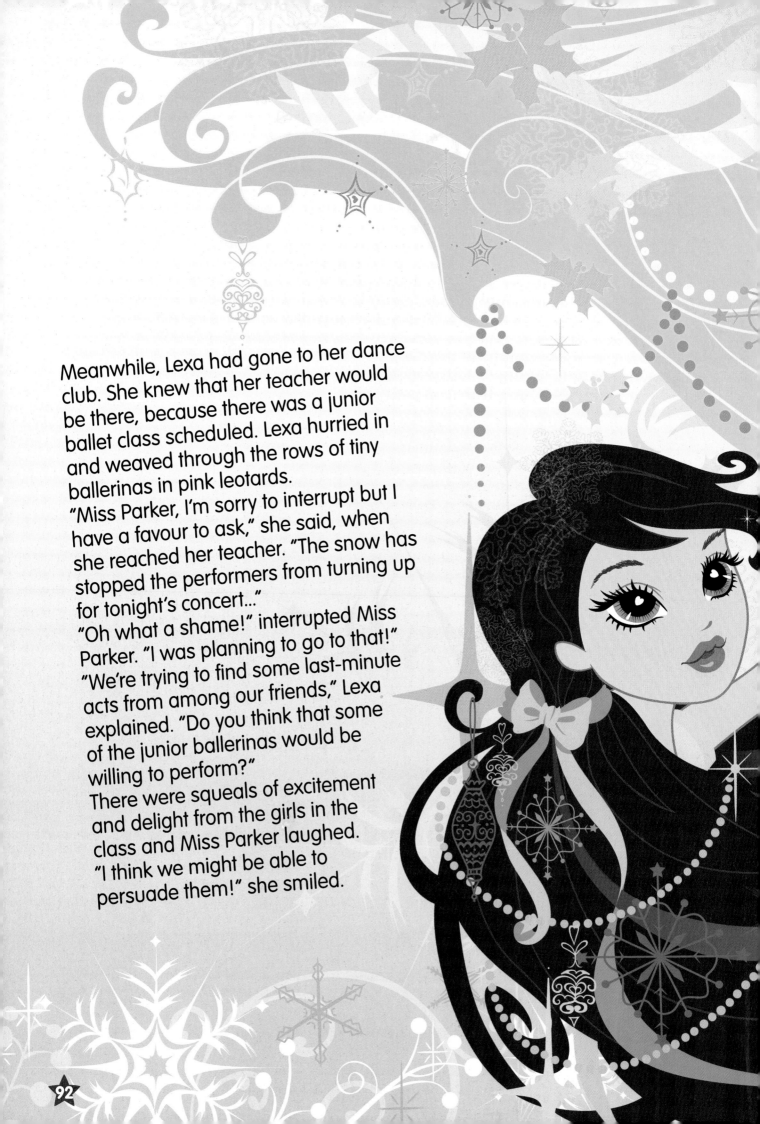

Meanwhile, Lexa had gone to her dance club. She knew that her teacher would be there, because there was a junior ballet class scheduled. Lexa hurried in and weaved through the rows of tiny ballerinas in pink leotards.

"Miss Parker, I'm sorry to interrupt but I have a favour to ask," she said, when she reached her teacher. "The snow has stopped the performers from turning up for tonight's concert..."

"Oh what a shame!" interrupted Miss Parker. "I was planning to go to that!"

"We're trying to find some last-minute acts from among our friends," Lexa explained. "Do you think that some of the junior ballerinas would be willing to perform?"

There were squeals of excitement and delight from the girls in the class and Miss Parker laughed. "I think we might be able to persuade them!" she smiled.

Meanwhile, Avery had visited her sports club. When she walked into the changing rooms, she saw the local gymnastics team getting changed, and a big smile spread over her face. "How do you guys fancy showing the whole of Riverlake what you can do?" she asked.

By the time the girls arrived back at Sophina's house, they had a long list of performers for the concert. Sophina's mum hugged them all.

"I can't believe that you've managed to save the concert," she said. "That's amazing."

"No, that's Moxie!" said Lexa.

The concert was being held at the town hall. That evening, despite the snow, crowds of people turned up. Some had already bought their tickets, and the rest were sold on the door. Sophina's mum even had to turn some people away!

Behind the scenes, there was a flurry of excited activity. Girls in white fluffy tutus dashed from the changing room to the make-up room. The magician was practising his act and pulling rainbow-coloured handkerchiefs from everyone's pockets, the violinists were tuning up and everyone was fizzing with energy.

Everyone except Sophina. She was sitting very quietly in the corner, trying to overcome her stage fright. She couldn't bear the thought of letting everyone down.

"I have to do this," she said to herself.

But the thought of the stage lights shining on her froze her with fear.

The concert began with the beautiful violin recital by the school music club. Then Lexa got everyone laughing with a perfectly timed comedy stand-up routine.

"She should be a comedian," Bria whispered to Avery backstage. "She's brilliant!"

Liam and Adam Connor played a selection of songs they had written themselves, and by the end of their performance, people were dancing in the aisles. They were followed by the ballerinas, who performed a scene from Swan Lake. Then the gymnasts sprang onto the stage, flipping and leaping. The audience oohed and aahed.

"I'm sure the original acts couldn't have got a better response!" said Sophina's mum happily.

At last it was time for Sophina, Bria and Avery to perform. They had agreed that Sophina would be the lead singer, while Bria and Avery were the backing singers. Sophina had been hoping that she would forget her nerves, but her legs were shaking.

"Come on, Sophina, it's your big moment!!" said Bria.

That made Sophina feel even worse. Her mouth felt dry.

"I can't," she said. "I can't go out on that stage and sing with everyone staring at me!"

"Sophina, you have a lovely voice," Avery pleaded.

Sophina was trembling.

She shook her head. Bria glanced at the stage.

"We'll have to do it alone," she said. "It won't be the same, though – oh!"

There was a loud clunk and the hall was plunged into darkness.

"The snow must have cut the power!" cried Lexa.

The girls could hear the people in the audience muttering and gasping.

"What now?" cried Bria in a panic.

Suddenly Sophina felt really calm. Her stage fright melted away. She knew exactly what to do. The stage was in blackness, but she felt her way out there, stood in the centre and took a deep breath.

Then she began to sing. As Sophina's voice soared through the hall, singing Silent Night, the audience fell quiet. No one could see anything, but Sophina's voice was steady and clear as a bell.

She heard the thrum of a guitar and smiled as music began to play – the Connor twins must have joined her on the stage! Then more voices joined in beside her... all the performers were stepping onto the stage and singing in the darkness! Gradually the audience joined in too, until the hall swelled with the sound of the beautiful carol. Sophina glanced at the hall windows and smiled. Thick snowflakes were still swirling down from the sky, but now she didn't mind the snow. She was with her friends, she was singing, and they had succeeded in raising the money that the children's charity needed.

This was going to be the happiest Christmas ever!

The End

Lexa's Guide to Fun and Games

© MGA

My best friends know that I love having fun, and I really enjoy playing games. Here are some of my all-time greatest activities!

© MGA

Dancing
I can't decide what is my favourite type of dancing! I love letting the music take hold of me and going wild, but I also adore salsa, ballroom and jive. Whatever the style, it's a great way to unwind, keep fit and get happy!

© MGA

Rounders
A summer day, a bunch of friends and a massive picnic – the perfect setting for a friendly game of rounders!

Cycling
Whether you're a fair-weather cyclist or a dedicated racer, you'll understand the thrill of using a bike to travel through the countryside. Exercise is addictive, and as you get fitter you will find yourself longing to get back in the saddle!

© MGA

Sleepovers

I absolutely love sleepovers! When I organise one with my friends, we just laugh the whole way through! Everyone suggests one game, we all bring our favourite snacks and we always end up staying up way too late. It's usually me who's keeping everyone awake at the end of the night, telling jokes!

Football

I love spending Sunday afternoons in the park with my friends. Someone always brings a football and we play girls v boys – awesome fun!

Comedy Club

Check the Internet and find out if there are any comedy clubs near you. Some of them have special events just for kids and teenagers. Who knows, you might be the first to spot a new comedy legend!

Theme Party

Of course, my all-time favourite activity is a fancy dress party. It has everything I love – music, crazy outfits, tons of friends and lots of dancing. Glow-sticks, tasty snacks, laughter, games and a live band would definitely make any party rock for me!

Horse Riding

If you have a riding stable close to where you live, a day of horse riding with your friends can be awesome fun. Some people are a bit scared of horses, but riding instructors are brilliant and will give the most nervous riders the gentlest horses.

What's your favourite way to relax?

Board Games

On sunny days I like being outside, but when it's cold and rainy, gathering around a board game is one of my favourite pastimes. Check out the board game we've designed for you to try on pages 28 and 29!

Snap

Of all the card games, this has got to be my favourite! I always get totally over-excited and shout "Snap" way too loud!

Bicycle Brainteaser

One sunny Saturday we all went on a bike ride. For fun, we decided to each take a different route to the picnic spot and race each other there. From these clues, can you figure out who won the race... and what happened along the way?

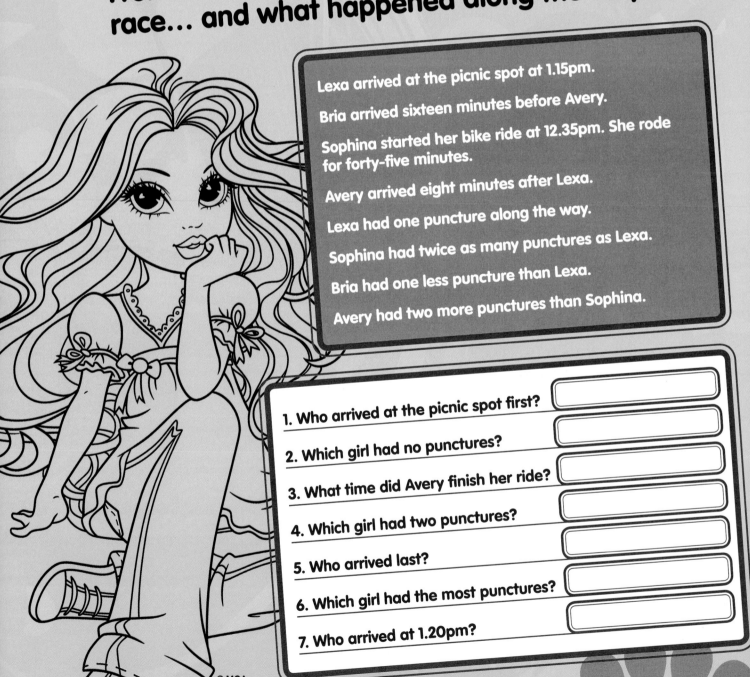

Lexa arrived at the picnic spot at 1.15pm.

Bria arrived sixteen minutes before Avery.

Sophina started her bike ride at 12.35pm. She rode for forty-five minutes.

Avery arrived eight minutes after Lexa.

Lexa had one puncture along the way.

Sophina had twice as many punctures as Lexa.

Bria had one less puncture than Lexa.

Avery had two more punctures than Sophina.

1. Who arrived at the picnic spot first?

2. Which girl had no punctures?

3. What time did Avery finish her ride?

4. Which girl had two punctures?

5. Who arrived last?

6. Which girl had the most punctures?

7. Who arrived at 1.20pm?

© MGA

Find Your Voice

If you're interested in creative writing like Avery, you have to be able to write in your own style, without copying anyone else. This is called finding your voice, and here's a great way to focus on your own unique style. It's called free writing.

You will need:
A pad of unlined paper.
Coloured pens.
A quiet place to write.

1. Open the pad in front of you and choose a colour to write in.

2. Close your eyes and focus on clearing your mind. Tell yourself that you are going to empty all your worries, thoughts and fears onto the paper.

3. Open your eyes and pick up a pen in your favourite colour. Place the tip of the pen on the paper. The pen should not leave the paper again until you have finished.

4. Start writing. Forget about the rules they teach you at school. Forget about punctuation and spelling – no one except you is going to read this.

5. It doesn't matter if what you write doesn't make perfect sense. It can be as rambling and crazy as a dream. This is all about freeing up some space in your mind.

6. There are no rules. You don't even have to write in straight lines.

7. Keep writing. Don't stop. If you can't think of anything to write, just write that you can't think of anything until another strand of thought comes to you.

8. You decide how long to write for. Set a timer for five, ten or fifteen minutes. When the timer goes off, read what you have written. If any ideas jump out at you, make a note of them.

9. Do a free-writing session every day. You will find that you are able to access a voice that is uniquely yours.

mince pies

We hope you'll try this recipe for our all-time favourite Christmas snacks!

Ingredients
110g butter
220g plain flour
Salt
Jar of mincemeat
Milk
Water
Icing sugar

Equipment
Large mixing bowl
One greased cake tray with twelve cake holes
Rolling pin
Pastry cutters
Wire rack
Sieve

© MGA

1. Preheat your oven to 200°C (Gas Mark 6).
2. Cut the butter into small cubes.
3. Use your fingertips to rub the butter into the flour, together with a pinch of salt. Do this from as high as possible to get air into the mixture.
4. Add a couple of tablespoons of water and blend the pastry into a ball. Add a little more water if necessary.
5. Wrap the pastry ball in cling film and put it into the fridge for thirty minutes.
6. Roll out the pastry on a floured surface.
7. Use a pastry cutter to cut a pastry circle large enough to fill one of the cake holes. It should be big enough to line the bottom and sides.
8. Spoon the mincemeat into the centre. Don't fill it up – a heaped teaspoon should be enough.
9. Brush the edges of the mince pie base with a little milk.
10. Using a slightly smaller pastry cutter, cut another pastry circle. This will be the lid of your mince pie.
11. Cover the mince pie with the lid, pressing the edges gently down.
12. Repeat steps 7–11 until you have used up all the pastry.
13. Brush the tops of the pies with milk and cut a small hole in the top of each pie.
14. Bake for twenty minutes or until the mince pies are golden brown.
15. Cool on a wire rack, and then use a small sieve to dust the mince pies with icing sugar.

Tip
If you have a star-shaped pastry cutter, you could make star-shaped lids for your mince pies!

The Real You

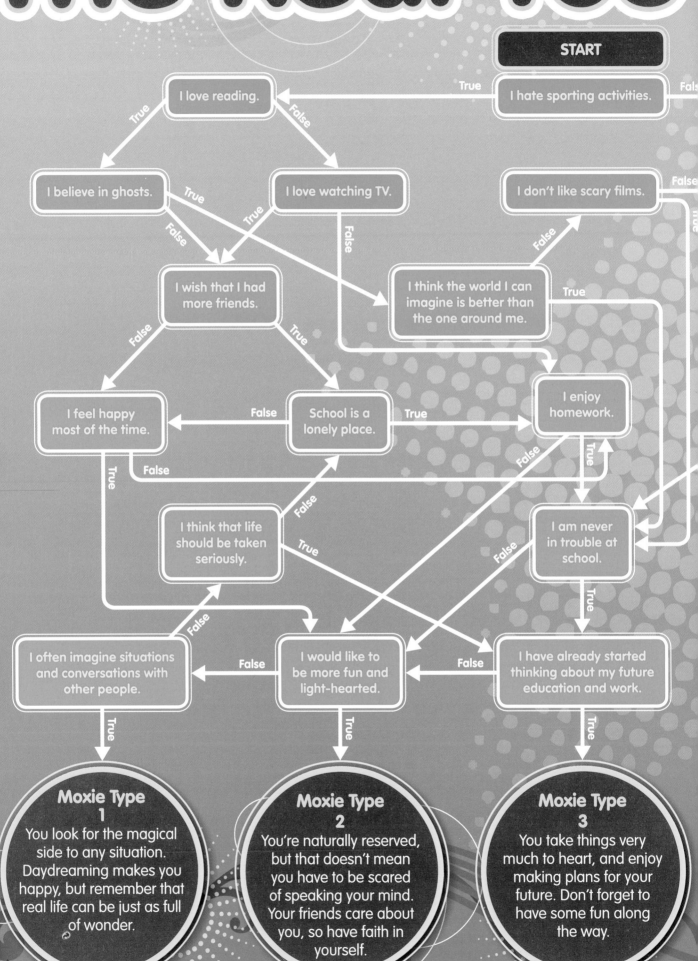

START

I hate sporting activities. — True → I love reading. / False

I love reading. — True → I believe in ghosts. / False → I love watching TV.

I don't like scary films. — False

I believe in ghosts. — True / False → I wish that I had more friends.

I love watching TV. — True → I wish that I had more friends. / False → I think the world I can imagine is better than the one around me.

I don't like scary films. — False / True

I think the world I can imagine is better than the one around me. — False

I wish that I had more friends. — False → I feel happy most of the time. / True → School is a lonely place.

I enjoy homework.

I feel happy most of the time. — True / False

School is a lonely place. — False → I feel happy most of the time. / True → I enjoy homework.

I enjoy homework. — True / False → I am never in trouble at school.

I think that life should be taken seriously. — False / True

I am never in trouble at school. — False / True

I often imagine situations and conversations with other people. — False / True

I would like to be more fun and light-hearted. — False / True

I have already started thinking about my future education and work. — False / True

Moxie Type 1
You look for the magical side to any situation. Daydreaming makes you happy, but remember that real life can be just as full of wonder.

Moxie Type 2
You're naturally reserved, but that doesn't mean you have to be scared of speaking your mind. Your friends care about you, so have faith in yourself.

Moxie Type 3
You take things very much to heart, and enjoy making plans for your future. Don't forget to have some fun along the way.

How well do you know yourself? How would you describe your personality to someone else?

Answer these questions and discover the real you!

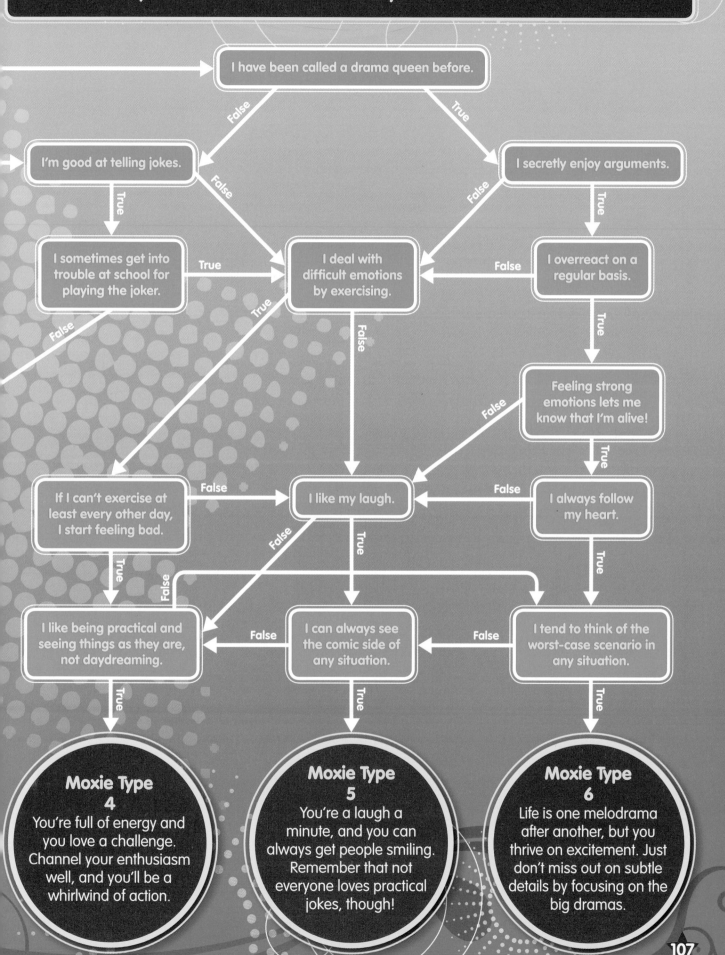

I have been called a drama queen before.

I'm good at telling jokes.

I secretly enjoy arguments.

I sometimes get into trouble at school for playing the joker.

I deal with difficult emotions by exercising.

I overreact on a regular basis.

Feeling strong emotions lets me know that I'm alive!

If I can't exercise at least every other day, I start feeling bad.

I like my laugh.

I always follow my heart.

I like being practical and seeing things as they are, not daydreaming.

I can always see the comic side of any situation.

I tend to think of the worst-case scenario in any situation.

Moxie Type 4
You're full of energy and you love a challenge. Channel your enthusiasm well, and you'll be a whirlwind of action.

Moxie Type 5
You're a laugh a minute, and you can always get people smiling. Remember that not everyone loves practical jokes, though!

Moxie Type 6
Life is one melodrama after another, but you thrive on excitement. Just don't miss out on subtle details by focusing on the big dramas.

Festive Drinks

These delicious drinks will cheer you and your friends on frosty days!

Be careful! Ask an adult to help you make these tasty drinks.

Christmas Chocolate

Ingredients
Milk
Bar of chocolate, grated
Marshmallows
Ground cinnamon
(Quantities will depend on how many mugs you are making!)

1. Heat the milk but do not allow it to boil.
2. Add the grated shaves of chocolate into the milk, whisking gently all the time.
3. When the milk is chocolatey enough for you, add a pinch of cinnamon and pour it into a mug.
4. Top with marshmallows and drink up!

Cranberry Cracker

Ingredients
2 cartons cranberry juice
1 carton orange juice
2 bottles of ginger ale
1 orange, sliced

Simply stir all the liquids together and add the sliced oranges. Delicious!

Taste Sensation

Ingredients
1 pint orange juice
1 pint apple juice
¼ pint water
½ tsp ground ginger
½ tsp mixed spice
½ tsp fresh ginger, finely grated
1 orange, sliced

1. In a large saucepan, combine the orange juice, apple juice, water, ginger and mixed spice.
2. Bring the mixture to the boil.
3. Simmer over a low heat for five minutes
4. Pour the warm punch into Christmas mugs and serve with slices of orange.

Festive Flavours

Ingredients
1 pint apple juice
4 cloves
½ stick of cinnamon
2 tbsp blackcurrant cordial
Sugar
1 apple, sliced

1. Combine the apple juice, cloves and cinnamon stick in a saucepan.
2. Heat gently for five minutes, but do not allow the mixture to boil.
3. Add the blackcurrant cordial and sugar to taste.
4. Cool the liquid in the fridge.
5. Strain the liquid and throw away the cloves and cinnamon pieces.
6. Pour into glasses and add slices of apple to garnish.

Answers:

Page 22
World of Words

Q	W	E	R	T	Y	U	I	O	P	A	S	D	F	G	H	D	H
J	K	L	Z	X	C	V	B	N	M	P	I	J	A	P	A	N	U
I	U	Y	T	R	E	W	Q	L	K	J	H	G	F	E	D	A	S
D	S	A	M	N	B	V	C	X	Z	Q	A	Z	X	R	S	L	W
W	Y	S	X	C	D	E	B	R	F	V	B	G	T	U	Y	I	H
N	M	L	J	U	I	H	K	L	T	A	N	Z	A	N	I	A	O
P	L	O	A	I	U	U	J	G	T	M	R	F	V	D	F	H	D
H	G	F	D	T	R	T	F	E	W	Q	A	X	K	X	E	T	R
L	K	J	A	H	I	G	R	F	D	S	I	L	R	N	T	B	Y
Q	W	N	E	W	Z	E	A	L	A	N	D	W	A	E	E	R	T
S	Y	D	F	G	H	J	N	N	U	B	N	V	M	W	B	C	Y
C	N	X	Z	A	S	D	C	E	S	W	I	P	N	O	I	I	K
J	A	H	T	P	Y	G	E	H	T	N	V	G	E	F	T	D	S
G	M	Z	X	C	V	B	N	M	R	L	K	J	D	H	G	O	F
F	R	D	S	A	I	C	E	L	A	N	D	W	E	R	C	T	Y
L	E	E	Y	H	G	F	R	T	L	B	C	D	D	I	M	K	I
G	G	R	E	R	E	W	D	S	I	C	B	G	X	V	G	T	Y
K	P	J	A	C	I	R	E	M	A	D	S	E	W	E	R	F	V
S	A	W	S	D	E	X	Z	A	T	Y	M	U	I	G	L	E	B

Page 23
Spot the Difference

© MGA

Page 26
Animal Challenge

Mystery animal: GIRAFFE

Page 27
Odd One Out
E.

Page 40
Colour Count
Guitar: 6 / Lollipop: 6 /
Lightening Flash: 4 /
Lightbulb: 7 / Banana: 6 /
Cupcake: 5

Page 41
Sweet Sudoku

6	7	5	8	3	9	4	2	1
2	9	3	1	4	6	5	7	8
8	4	1	7	5	2	3	9	6
1	6	4	9	8	5	7	3	2
3	5	9	2	6	7	8	1	4
7	8	2	3	1	4	6	5	9
4	2	7	6	9	3	1	8	5
5	3	8	4	2	1	9	6	7
9	1	6	5	7	8	2	4	3

Page 44
True or False
1. False / 2. True / 3. True /
4. False / 5. True / 6. True /
7. False / 8. False / 9. False /
10. True / 11. False / 12. True /
13. True / 14. True / 15. False

Page 45
Avery's Amazing Adventure

Page 62-63
Devastating Detective Skills
1. In bunches / 2. Yellow /
3. Orange / 4. Avery /
5. Cherries / 6. Blue / 7. Four /
8. Avery / 9. Pink / 10. Sophina /
Bonus Question: Avery

Page 84
Snack Patterns

Page 102
Bicycle Brainteaser
1. Bria / 2. Bria / 3. 1.23pm /
4. Sophina / 5. Avery /
6. Avery / 7. Sophina